Super Cat Speed!

Based on the screenplay
"Catboy's Great Gig"

Ready-to-Read

Simon Spotlight
New York London Toronto Sydney New Delhi

SIMON SPOTLIGHT
An imprint of Simon & Schuster Children's Publishing Division
1230 Avenue of the Americas, New York, New York 10020
This Simon Spotlight edition December 2017
Adapted by Cala Spinner from the series PJ Masks

Manufactured in the United States of America 1117 LAK
10 9 8 7 6 5 4 3 2 1
ISBN 978-1-5344-0926-2 (hc)
ISBN 978-1-5344-0925-5 (pbk)
ISBN 978-1-5344-0927- 9 (eBook)

The school concert

is tomorrow.

But where are

the instruments?

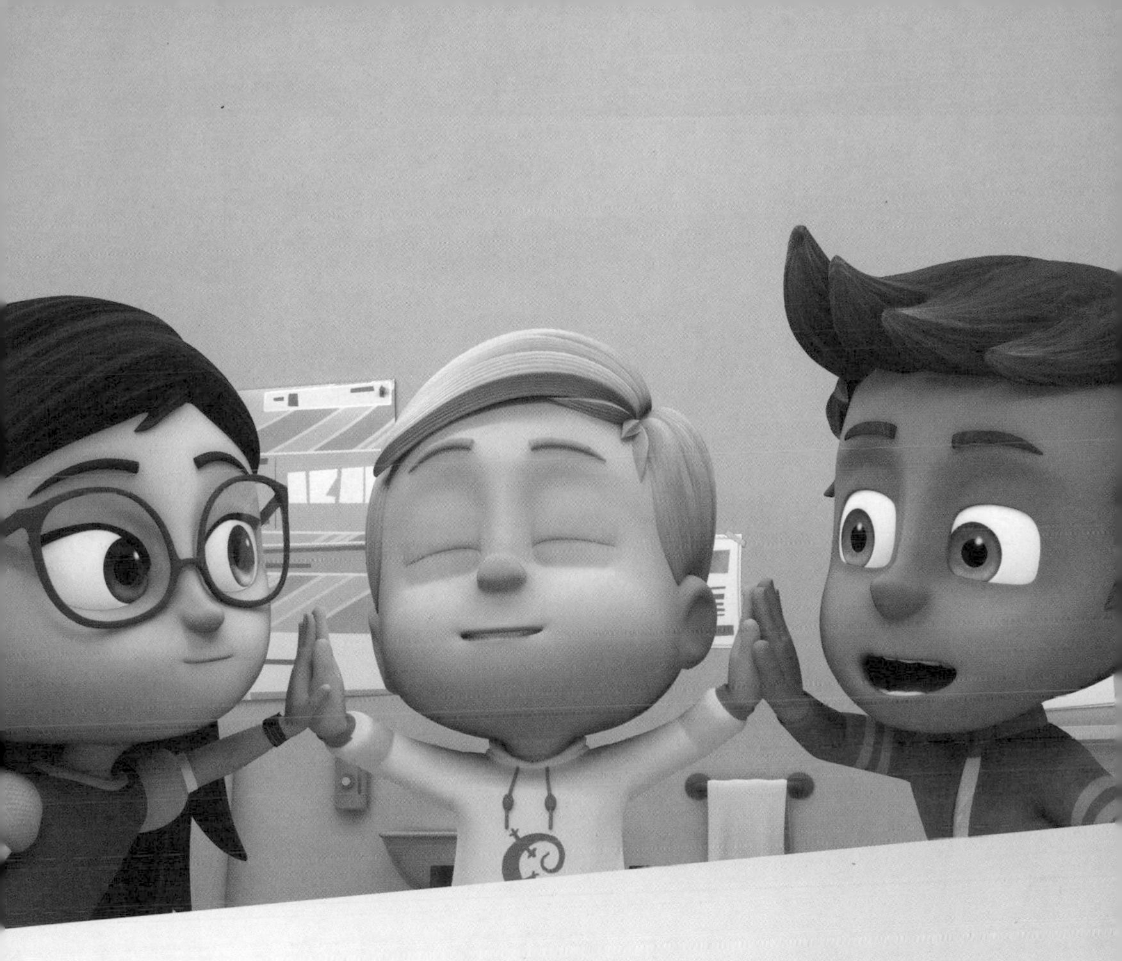

This is a job
for the PJ Masks!

Amaya becomes Owlette!

Greg becomes Gekko!

Connor becomes Catboy!

They are the PJ Masks!

Catboy is scared.
He does not want
to play in the concert.
What if he messes up?

The PJ Masks hear
a harsh noise.

It is Night Ninja!

Night Ninja is singing.

The Ninjalinos have the missing instruments.

Catboy will use his
Super Cat Leap
to trap the Ninjalinos
with a net.

But he is too afraid.

It does not work.

“If we cannot get
the instruments back,
I guess the concert
is off,” says Owlette.

Catboy does not like to see his friend sad.

Catboy uses Super Cat Speed!

He speeds around

the Ninjalinos.

He takes back one of

the instruments.

It is a recorder.

Catboy will need to
play the recorder.
Everyone is watching,
but Catboy must be brave.

Catboy plays the recorder.

He is really good!

The Ninjalinos like
playing with Catboy
more than Night Ninja.

They leave Night Ninja!

Then Owlette and Gekko trap Night Ninja in a drum.

The Ninjalinos give
the instruments back.
“I will get you for this!”
Night Ninja says.

PJ Masks all shout hooray!
Because in the night,
we saved the day!

Catboy learned that

it is okay to be afraid,

but always do your best!